PUFFIN BOOKS

SEPTIMOUSE, SUPERMOUSE!

Ann Jungman was born in London in 1938, the daughter of German Jewish refugees. Having done some supply teaching at an all-girls school whilst studying Law, Ann decided to do a year of post-graduate teacher training. She then spent a year in Israel, first working on a Kibbutz and later as a secretary in Tel Aviv. She taught for six years in a variety of Inner London schools, before stopping to do an MA in American Studies, Literature and Comparative Education at London University.

Ann had written several stories for children while teaching, many of them about dragons and ghosts, princesses and vampires. In 1982, after many rejections and many years, *Vlad the Drac* was finally accepted by a small publisher. Its popularity and success enabled Ann to settle down and write full time. She has spent many years in Australia but now lives in London.

By the same author

THERE'S A TROLL AT THE BOTTOM OF MY GARDEN
SEPTIMOUSE . . . BIG CHEESE

ANN JUNGMAN

SEPTIMOUSE, SUPERMOUSE!

ILLUSTRATED BY SAMI SWEETEN

PUFFIN BOOKS

For Sophie, Georgia and Sean

PUFFIN BOOKS

Published by the Penguin Group
Penguin Books Ltd, 27 Wrights Lane, London W8 5TZ, England
Penguin Books USA Inc., 375 Hudson Street, New York, New York 10014, USA
Penguin Books Australia Ltd, Ringwood, Victoria, Australia
Penguin Books Canada Ltd, 10 Alcorn Avenue, Toronto, Ontario, Canada M4V 3B2
Penguin Books (NZ) Ltd, 182–190 Wairau Road, Auckland 10, New Zealand

Penguin Books Ltd, Registered Offices: Harmondsworth, Middlesex, England

First published by Viking 1991
Published in Puffin Books 1993
10 9 8 7 6 5 4 3

Text copyright © Ann Jungman, 1991
Illustrations copyright © Sami Sweeten, 1991
All rights reserved

The moral right of the author has been asserted

Filmset in Palatino (Linotron)

Printed in England by Clays Ltd, St Ives plc

Contents

Seven Little Mice

"I'm a genius," yelled Mr Mouse, leaping into the air. "I'm the greatest. I'm number one. I'm a super plus, wonderful, brilliant mouse."

"Whatever are you so excited about?" asked Mrs Mouse. "Just because we now have seven new, lovely little mice is no reason for carrying on like this."

"My love, my love, you don't understand. We have just produced seven little boy mice."

"That is correct," replied his wife, nodding.

"Well, this little one," said Mr Mouse, proudly picking up one of the new-born mice, "is a very, *very* special little mouse."

"They are all special, my love," said Mrs Mouse reprovingly.

"Of course they are, but this one is extra special because, my love, he is the seventh son of a seventh son. I was my parents' seventh son and he is ours."

"Yes, but what does *that* mean?" demanded Mrs Mouse suspiciously.

"It means, my love, that he will have magical powers. He will be able to do things other mice cannot."

"What kind of things?"

"I don't know, my love, we will have to wait and see. Time alone will tell, but one way or another I am sure he will be quite remarkable. Now, what are we going to call these little mice?"

"How about John, James, Julius, Joseph, Jeremy, Jack and Joshua?"

"Very nice, my love, wonderful names.
But I think our seventh should not be
called Joshua but Septimus."

"Why Septimus?" asked Mrs Mouse.

"Because," replied her husband
proudly, "it means the seventh."

"Hmm," said Mrs Mouse thinking hard.
"I think that as he is a mouse he should be
called Septimouse."

"Perfect, wonderful, brilliant," shouted
Mr Mouse doing cartwheels all over the
mousehold. "Septimouse he shall be and I
have no doubt that he will bring great
good fortune to us all."

For the first weeks of their lives,
Septimouse and his six brothers played
happily in the mouse hole until one day
Mrs Mouse noticed Septimouse
dangerously near the exit of the hole.

"We shall have to tell them this
evening," Mrs Mouse told her husband.
"If we leave it any longer it may be too
late."

"Very well, my love. Tonight after supper we will give them the Mouse Talk. You are quite right, we can't be too careful."

So that night after the seven mice had eaten, Mr Mouse sat them in a circle at his feet.

"Now, my little ones, I want you to listen very carefully to what I am going to say, for what I am about to tell you is the most important lesson a mouse can learn. You must never, ever, *ever* touch a piece of cheese."

"What is cheese?" asked Julius.

"Cheese is food. It is yellow and delicious and the most wonderful dish a mouse can have, but you must never, *never* touch it."

"Why not?" demanded Septimouse.

"Because the big people use it to trap us. They put cheese in their traps because they know that we can't resist it."

"Who are the big people?" asked James.

"The big people are the rulers of the whole world," said his father. "They are very odd creatures. They walk on two legs and they have no fur. You never saw anything so strange. Unfortunately, they don't like mice, so you must always stay away from them if you can."

"Where do the big people get this wonderful cheese stuff from?" asked Septimouse.

"You do ask the oddest questions," replied his father. "I have no idea. Why do you ask?"

"Because if it is the most delicious thing in the world for a mouse, then I think we should all have some. I shall go and ask the big people how they get their cheese and then we can have some of our own."

"No, Septimouse!" cried his mother. "Promise me you won't try to do such a thing. The big people hate us; if you went into their world you would never come back."

"Your mother is quite right, Septimouse. I mean, even if you managed to escape (for as the seventh son of a seventh son you well might), you couldn't find out their secrets. You see, the big people don't speak mouse language. They have this funny booming way of talking. It's very ugly and *we* can't do it."

"I can," said Septimouse. "Listen!" And to the amazement of his parents and his brothers he said in big person language:

"Could you tell me, please, from where do you get your cheese?"

"I told you he'd be special," cried Mr Mouse, leaping up and down. "Didn't I say on the day he was born that this mouse would be special? Talking like a big person, well, that really is something."

14

"Septimouse, Septimouse my son," said Mrs Mouse, weeping. "Promise me that you won't try and talk to the big people. Just because you can doesn't mean you must."

"Mother," said Septimouse calmly. "Please don't worry about me. All will be well. Nothing ever happens to the seventh son of a seventh son. I will go and talk to the big people and find out where they get this cheese stuff and then we can all have as much as we want."

"Septimouse, you don't understand. The big people are our enemies, they don't like mice and they do away with as many of us as they can."

"Why are they our enemies?" demanded Septimouse.

"I'm not sure," replied his father. "It's just always been so."

"Well, I think it's time a mouse went and tried to find out what it is all about.

Maybe we don't have to be enemies of the big people for ever and ever."

Mrs Mouse burst into tears and Mr Mouse put his arm around her.

"It's no good, my love, the boy is determined to go and we must wish him luck. Just one thing, Septimouse. The *little* big people are not as unkind to mice as the *big* big people. So on this first trip, find yourself a *little* big person to talk to."

"Father, I shall do as you say. Mother, farewell. Brothers, I shall see you in the morning. Don't worry about me. As soon as I've got the information I need I shall be back. See you later, everyone." And he disappeared through the mouse hole into the big people's house.

Little Big Person

Septimouse stepped out of the mouse hole into a new world. He looked around him in amazement. Everything was huge and towered over him.

"Hmm," he thought. "The big people must be very big indeed. How interesting it will be to actually see one of these giants."

The little mouse padded across the kitchen and peeped round the door. Seeing nothing he slipped into the hallway. With horror he looked at the big flight of stairs.

"I hope I can find the little big people without going up there," he thought to himself. Just then he heard a sound from behind him. Septimouse looked round and

saw a large, furry animal with a long tail
looking at him in an unkind way.

"Oh dear!" thought the mouse. "*That*
can't be a big person because it has four
legs and fur. I wonder what it *can* be? Well,
whatever it is, it isn't friendly."

The great red, furry monster approached
Septimouse, twitching its whiskers and
narrowing its eyes to little yellow slits.

"O creature of the night," cried
Septimouse, staring hard at the terrible

furry monster and pointing at it with his right front paw, "I, Septimouse, the seventh son of a seventh son, do command you to be still."

The furry creature suddenly froze and stood on the spot unable to move.

"That's better," said Septimouse. "Now, creature of the night, I, Septimouse, the seventh son of a seventh son, command you to speak but not to move."

"Miaow . . ." said the creature in a wounded tone.

"Miaow," replied Septimouse.

"You can speak cat-talk!" said the furry monster. "How did you learn that?"

"Oh, I can do pretty much anything," the mouse told him. "Cat-talk you say? Hmm. Then you must be a cat."

"Well, of course I'm a cat. What did you think I was, a lion? Now please, take the spell off so that I can move."

"Not so fast, my friend. How do I know that if I lift the spell you won't do something nasty?"

"I give you my word, a cat's word of honour."

"Something tells me that you're not to be trusted. Perhaps you should tell me all about cats."

"With pleasure," agreed the cat. "Cats are wonderful creatures. Clever, beautiful, athletic, clean and, above all, very friendly to mice. The most important thing you need to know about a cat is that they like mice more than anything in the world. Now that you know, oh seventh son of a seventh son, please take the spell away, so that I can move and we can play and have fun together."

"You should know better than to try and fool the seventh son of a seventh son, for when we hear a lie our whiskers seem to burn at the ends. I do not believe that cats are friends of us mice. Now tell me the truth, or I will turn you into a stone cat in twenty seconds."

"No, don't!" shrieked the cat. "It was a lie. Well, it sort of was. You see, we cats do like mice more than anything. We like to chase them and then eat them. It's not our fault, it's just our nature."

"I see," nodded Septimouse. "Just as we mice can't resist cheese, you can't resist mice."

"That's about the size of it," agreed the cat.

"I'll make a deal with you," offered the mouse. "I'll take the spell off you and you will be able to move about and run and leap and jump, but you mustn't try to catch me or you will be turned into a stone cat for ever and ever. Do you agree?"

"Not much choice," moaned the cat. "I

agree, but only on condition that you don't go telling the other cats, or none of them will want to know me."

"You mean there are more of you furry monsters?"

"Yeah, masses of us."

"In this house?"

"Oh no, not in this house. This is *my* house."

"I see. Very well then. I, Septimouse, the seventh son of a seventh son, am willing to give you back, oh cat, your power to run and jump and climb. But I charge you to remember that this is only on condition that you never again, in your whole life, chase a mouse. Do you agree?"

"I do."

Septimouse held up his right paw again and said in a dramatic tone:

"I, Septimouse, the seventh son of a seventh son, say let the cat be able to move again."

The cat twitched his whiskers and then shook his head.

"I can move, I can move! Oh, thank you, Septimouse, thank you for not turning me into a statue. My name's Oscar and I'm very grateful. Now, you tell me what you're doing here and maybe I can help."

"I want to find out about cheese," explained the mouse. "I want to know where the big people get it from. Then us mice can get it from the same place and have as much as we like without getting into trouble. My mother and father say that I should find a little big person and they might help me."

"A little big person?" muttered the cat, looking puzzled. "Oh, you mean a *child*. Well, yes, we've got one of them here. She's called Katie. Would you like to meet her?"

"I most certainly would, Oscar, that is most kind of you."

"Well, you have to go all the way up those stairs and it's the second door on the right."

Septimouse looked up at the flight of stairs.

"Oscar, I can't go up there without a ladder, I'm just too small."

"Not to worry, jump on my back and we'll have you there in two seconds."

So Septimouse climbed on to his friend's back and Oscar raced up the stairs and into

Katie's bedroom. Of course, like everyone else in the house she was fast asleep. Oscar leapt on to the bed and Septimouse climbed down from his back and walked over to Katie's sleeping head on the pillow. Gently he pulled her hair.

Katie slowly opened her eyes and saw the mouse looking at her very hard.

"Don't cry, little big person," said the mouse. "It is only I, Septimouse, and I need your help."

Katie stared at him through the dim glow of her night-light.

"You can talk!" she whispered.

"Of course I can, for I am the seventh son of a seventh son and have magical powers. Now, I need your help, little big person Katie."

"How did you know my name?"

"Oscar told me."

"My cat! So you can talk to him too?"

"I certainly can and will happily give him any messages you might wish to send. Now, little big person – down to business. I want to learn all about cheese. You see, we mice absolutely *love* cheese, but it often gets us into trouble. Now, I thought that if I could get cheese for the mice in the same way as you big people get it, then maybe we won't get into trouble."

"I don't know anything about cheese, except that it's made from milk."

"Milk is yummy," chipped in Oscar.

"What is milk?" asked Septimouse.

"Come on," said Katie. "We'll go

downstairs and I'll show you. Come on, into my pocket."

So the three of them went downstairs. Very quietly, Katie opened the fridge.

"Look," she said. "This is milk."

"Could I try a little?" asked Septimouse. "If that wouldn't be an awful lot of trouble."

Katie poured some into a saucer and put it on the kitchen table and Septimouse sipped it.

"Very nice," he decided. "Very nice indeed."

"Can I finish it off?" asked Oscar.

"What is he saying?" asked Katie.

"He wants to finish it off."

Katie put it on the floor and the cat lapped away.

"Would you by any chance have a bit of cheese?" asked the mouse. "You see, I've heard so much about it but I have never tasted even a morsel."

Katie got out the big plastic cheese dish and opened it. Septimouse stood on his hind legs and peeped in.

"Oh, it smells super delicious. Which bit is cheese?"

"They're all cheese. There are lots of different kinds. Wait a minute and I'll cut you a bit of each."

Soon Septimouse was sampling all the cheeses and licking his whiskers with delight.

"Oh, they are wonderful, each one is more delicious than the last. Yes, I must definitely find a safe way to have cheese every day. Where do the big people get this cheese?"

"We buy it from a shop," Katie told him. "And the shops get it from dairies and cheese factories, who make it from milk."

"But *how* do they make it from milk?"

"I'm not sure, but I can find out for you. I'll go to the library and get a book out

about cheese-making. If you come back tomorrow night I'll be waiting for you."

"Books. What odd words you use. What are books?"

"You'll see tomorrow night. Now off you go because I'm very tired. Here, take a bit more cheese and I'll see you then."

Katie went up to bed yawning, Oscar curled up in his basket and Septimouse ran happily back to the mouse hole.

"Septimouse!" cried Mr Mouse. "You made it, you are back, the big people didn't get you. Heaven be praised."

"Father, mother and brothers, I am happy to tell you that I think I have found out how we can get lots of cheese."

Mrs Mouse dried her eyes and rushed to put her arms around Septimouse.

"Never mind about the cheese, my boy. It's not important. But your safety is."

"Mother, you mustn't worry so. For tonight I not only made friends with little big person Katie, but also she has agreed to help us. She is getting me a book about cheese-making."

"Well!" gasped Mrs Mouse. "Wonders will never cease."

"This is truly amazing," agreed her husband. "I knew we would see great things from a seventh son of a seventh son, but I never dreamed he would actually make friends with a big person, not even a little one."

"And tonight, Father," said Septimouse, "is only the beginning."

The following night, Septimouse was
getting ready to go and see Katie and read
the book. He was just going to walk out of
the mouse hole when a voice came
through the gap. Septimouse heard his
friend Oscar calling him.

"Septimouse, where are you? Aren't you
coming out to play with me tonight? I'll be
very, very good – I promise."

What his family heard was "Miaow".

Septimouse called back to Oscar:

"Coming in a minute, Oscar. Just got to say goodnight to my mum and dad and six brothers."

What his family heard was Septimouse saying "Miaow".

"Don't go," shrieked Mr Mouse. "It's a cat!"

"It's all right, Dad, it's only my friend Oscar," Septimouse told them. "He won't harm me, he just wants to play."

"You've never made friends with a cat!" exclaimed his father. "That's just not possible."

"Yes it is," Septimouse assured him. "You see, being the seventh son of a seventh son, I can not only talk to big people but also to cats." And he gave a big "Miaow" meaning "I'm coming", and ran out of the mouse hole leaving his family with their mouths hanging open.

"Glad to see you, Septimouse," said

Oscar. "Maybe I'll get another saucer of milk. Up on my back. Little big person Katie is waiting for you."

Soon they were both on Katie's bed.

"Hello, Septimouse," she said. "Look, here's the book. It tells us how to make cheese and there are lots of pictures to help."

Septimouse looked at the book with interest.

"So *that's* a book, is it?" he muttered, and sitting on the page he began to read it.

"You can read too!" commented Katie. "You really are a very unusual mouse."

"Am I?" said Septimouse. "Well, it must be because I am the seventh son of a seventh son."

"You know, all that seventh son of a seventh son stuff is a bit of a mouthful and you seem to have to say it a lot. Why don't we shorten it to S.S.S.S. or 4S?"

"Good idea," agreed Septimouse. "Now, I need to make a few notes and a few sketches and take them back down to the mouse hole."

"Whatever for?" asked Katie.

"Little big person Katie, how am I going to make cheese in my mouse hole if we don't have the right machines?"

"You mean you're going to make cheese in this house?"

"Of course," replied Septimouse.

"How will you get the milk you need?"

"That is of course a big problem. Where

do you get your milk from?"

"We buy it in a shop," explained Katie. "Or otherwise the milkman delivers it."

"What does 'buy' mean?" asked the mouse.

"You go to a place that has a lot of what you want and you take what you need and then you pay for it with money. Look, this is money."

"Hmm," muttered Septimouse. "How would a mouse get hold of money?"

"Miaow," said Oscar loudly.

"What does he want?" asked Katie.

"He wants to know when he's going to get his saucer of milk in exchange for bringing me up here."

"It's very odd knowing what Oscar is saying," commented Katie. "Ask him about money. He might have some ideas."

So Septimouse told Oscar about the problem.

"Oh, that's easily solved," sniffed Oscar. "People are always leaving money lying around. I always see it on the floor and out in the garden – people drop it all over the place and don't even notice. Don't think much of it myself. You can't eat it, it's too hard and it tastes awful. Now come on, what about my milk?"

"Oscar says there is lots of money just lying around on the ground. If that's the case I shall alert all the mice and they must look for money and when they find it they must bring it to me. Then I will give it to you and you can go and get milk for me

from the shop place you talk about. Would you do that?"

"Yes, of course."

"What's happening?" moaned Oscar. "When am I going to get my saucer of milk?"

"In a minute, Oscar. Little big person Katie and I are arranging to buy milk for my cheese factory," Septimouse explained.

"Buy milk!" exclaimed Oscar. "No need to buy it. Just take it from the doorstep in the morning, after the milkman has been."

"No," declared Septimouse. "That would be stealing. We'll only use milk that we can pay for."

"If I get all the cats to help you look for money," said Oscar, "what would you give us in return?"

"In return for your help," said Septimouse, "you cats can have cream. I read in the book here that cream is also made from milk. Every cat that helps us with money will get cream. Do you think you can get the cats to help?"

"I can try," answered Oscar. "Problem is, us cats love to chase mice. It's such fun, you see. I might have a problem getting them to agree not to do it."

"I know," said Septimouse. "The cats can chase mice, but if they catch them they must let them go. For every mouse that is caught and spared the cat will get an extra helping of cream. But if any cat harms a mouse, that cat will be turned to stone on the spot. You can tell them, Oscar, that I, Septimouse, the seventh son of a seventh son, can and *will* do that."

"I'll give it a whirl," said Oscar. "Now, please, how about my milk?"

"Oscar wants his milk," Septimouse told Katie. "And I would like just the tiniest bit of cheese, then I will leave you to sleep. Little big person, you have been a great help. There is not a mouse in the district who will not be grateful."

When Oscar had drunk his milk and Septimouse had nibbled a bit of cheese and got a little piece for his mother, father and each of his six brothers, it was time to part.

"See you soon," called Septimouse, waving as he ran towards the mouse hole. "I'll be in touch about buying the milk once I have made the machines for my cheese factory. Get the cats looking for money, Oscar. Byeee."

Bones

As soon as Septimouse got back to the mouse hole he laid out his sketches.

"These," he announced, "are my plans for the cheese factory, the factory that will provide mice with as much cheese as they want without falling into the big people's traps."

Mr Mouse studied the plans for a few minutes and then smiled broadly and declared:

"It doesn't look difficult at all. Don't worry, Septimouse, your brothers and I will build the factory. It's a great idea, that's what it is."

"Thank you, Father. If you take care of that side of things, I will go and find the local mice and tell them of our plans."

So while Mr and Mrs Mouse and John, James, Julius, Joseph, Jeremy and Jack sawed and glued and banged nails, Septimouse ran off to search for the other mice.

"That boy is so rash," said Mrs Mouse. "Out in the street indeed. He could meet any number of cats or even dogs!"

"I don't think you need worry about him, my love," said her husband proudly. "That lad can clearly take care of himself."

Outside, Septimouse was talking to Oscar the cat.

"I need your help, Oscar. I'm looking for mice. Have you any idea where I can find the mice in this street?"

Oscar laughed loudly.

"If there's one thing I do know it's where to find mice. House numbers 44, 57, 63, 11, 36, 25, 27, and let me see now – oh yes, number 78. Going visiting, are you? Do you want me to come with you, Septimouse?"

"No thanks, Oscar, it would just alarm the mice if you came."

"You might need me to protect you against the other cats."

"No need to worry. I'll be all right because I can deal with cats in my 4S way."

"Well get on with it then," sniffed Oscar, "because I am waiting for my first plate of thick, silky, delicious cream."

Septimouse ran off to the houses Oscar had named, telling the mice that they were all invited to a midnight cheese party at his cheese factory the following week.

"But Septimouse, what about cats and dogs?" squeaked the mice. "If we go out

46

into the street we are in terrible danger. We might never arrive at your cheese factory."

"Fear not!" Septimouse told them. "For I am the seventh son of a seventh son and have magical powers. I will see to it that you are not troubled by cats or what are the others called?"

"Dogs," squeaked the mice. "They are even bigger and noisier than cats. Dogs are very terrible indeed."

"I'll sort them out whatever they are, before the cheese party. Never fear. The street will be cat and dog free on the night of the party. You have my 4S word for it."

The following night, Septimouse stuck his head out of the mouse hole.

"Psst, Oscar, where are you? Come here."

Oscar yawned and stretched out.

"I'm asleep, Septi, old boy."

"Well, wake up. I need you to take me to little big person Katie. I have to talk to her about dogs."

"Dogs!" snorted Oscar. "Why do you want to talk to her about *them*?"

"Because I am planning a Grand Cheese Party for all the mice and they are scared the dogs will attack them on their way to the party."

"What about us cats?" declared Oscar indignantly. "Aren't they afraid of us?"

"Of course they are," Septimouse assured him. "Only I'm relying on you to tell the cats about my terrible magical powers. You must go and warn them all that if they harm even the whisker of a single mouse, I will turn them to stone. If, however, they are good, they will all get lashings of cream."

"I'll tell 'em, Septi, old chap, don't worry. Oscar will spread the word."

"Good, now if you'd be so kind as to

take me upstairs, Oscar, I'd be very grateful.''

A few minutes later Septimouse was whispering in Katie's ear.

''Sorry to bother you, little big person Katie, but I need your help again.''

''What sort of help?'' asked Katie sleepily.

''Do you have any of this money stuff, little big person Katie?''

''A bit,'' mumbled Katie. ''What do you want it for?''

"I need it to buy milk for my cheese factory. You see, I have invited all the mice to a cheese party to show them the factory. Now, when they see that we really can make cheese, they will go looking for money. Then we can pay for the milk ourselves. But this first time I need a loan from you. I will pay it back very quickly on my honour as a seventh son of a seventh son."

"Of course, Septimouse, that's fine. I'd love to help. Now you wait there. I'll get my money-box and we'll see how much I've got."

Septimouse watched fascinated as Katie counted the money.

"Have we got enough?" he asked anxiously.

"Yes, plenty," she told him.

"Would there be enough for something else?"

"Depends what it is."

"I'm not sure what it is either, little big person. You see, the mice are scared of some terrible beast called a dog. Now, what I need to know is, what it is that dogs can't resist. You know, in the way mice can't resist cheese and cats can't resist cream and mice."

"Bones," Katie told him. "Dogs love bones."

"These bones, little big person, are they expensive?"

"Oh no," said Katie. "They are very cheap. I can get lots from the butcher."

"I see. Well, little big person, would you go and buy me these bones and some milk. And we also need something called rennet that turns the milk into cheese."

"Of course I will, Septimouse. You won't need very much milk, if you only need mice-sized pieces. I'll leave a pint outside your mouse hole tonight."

"Little big person, you are wonderful. One day I will repay not only your money but all your help."

"I'm sure you will," muttered Katie, as she fell asleep again.

Shrinking

The next night the mouse family scampered out of their mouse hole and there stood a carton of milk.

"But how will we get it through the mouse hole?" asked Mrs Mouse.

Septimouse stood in front of the carton, raised his front paws and closed his eyes.

"Milk carton, I, Septimouse, the seventh son of a seventh son, do hereby command you to shrink."

The mice all stared at the carton with fascination. For a moment nothing happened and then before their very eyes it began to shrink.

"Hurrah!" they shouted. "Good for you, Septimouse." And they all helped to push the carton into the mouse hole.

The mouse family poured the milk into the cheese-making machine. Mr Mouse put the lid on and they left the milk to turn into cheese.

"Well," said Mr Mouse. "Now all we have to do is add the rennet and wait. Septimouse, my son, I think the party can go ahead."

"Only one problem remains," announced Septimouse dramatically. "Dogs!"

"Dogs?" questioned his mother.

"Yes. You remember you told me that if the mice from the other houses had to come out into the street to get to our party, they might be attacked by dogs? Well, I have a plan to deal with these terrible monsters. I shall go out into the street and tame the beasts." And he walked grandly through the mouse hole.

"Be careful, my boy!" cried his father.

"Come back," wept his mother. "Oh

Septimouse, my brave, brave son."

Taking no notice of his parents' cries, Septimouse ran out of the mouse hole.

"Oscar," he called. "Come and show me a dog."

"Sorry, Septimouse, old boy. I can't do that. I'm scared of dogs."

"Well then, just come over to the window here and point to one."

Oscar climbed up on the window-sill of the kitchen window and then pulled Septimouse up. Together they peered out.

"There!" said Oscar, pointing to a huge spaniel barking loudly.

"Oh dear," sighed Septimouse. "Dogs really are so big and noisy."

"Will you turn her into a stone?" asked Oscar. "Like you did to me?"

"No, I think not. I have another plan for that dog. You stay here and watch. Septimouse the Great is about to perform another amazing feat."

Septimouse went into the street and walked determinedly towards the barking dog.

"Dog," he called, staring hard at the dog. "I, Septimouse, the seventh son of a seventh son, do command you to shrink."

As the spaniel began to get smaller and smaller, Septimouse breathed a sigh of relief. Out of the corner of his eye, Septimouse could see Oscar, holding his hands up over his head like a boxer, cheering.

"Woof," cried the dog miserably. "I'm getting smaller, oh woof, help, help!"

"Don't worry, dog," Septimouse told her. "Woof, woof, I'll make you big again, after we've had a chat."

"You're a mouse," commented the dog.

"Correct," agreed Septimouse.

"Why did you make me so small?" demanded the dog. "I don't like it, I don't feel safe."

"Calm down, dog," said Septimouse. "I need your help. Once you agree I'll make you dog-sized in a second. You see, I have just built a cheese factory."

"So?" sniffed the dog.

"Well, I am planning a cheese party for all the local mice to launch my cheese factory," explained Septimouse.

"So?" muttered the dog. "Dogs don't like cheese."

"I know," agreed Septimouse. "But dogs do frighten mice. Now, what I want you to promise is that you won't frighten any mice on their way to my party."

"Not even one little one?" asked the dog wistfully.

"No, not even one," insisted Septimouse. "But I will give you a lovely, juicy bone instead. Do you agree?"

"Done!" yelled the dog.

"Good. Now listen, dog. I will make you big again if you agree to tell every other dog in the area about Septimouse and his magical powers of shrinkage and his offer of juicy bones. Do you agree?"

"Of course I agree. Woof. Yes, definitely."

Septimouse closed his eyes and held out his arms in front of him.

"I, Septimouse, the seventh son of a seventh son, command you to grow and be dog-sized again."

As Septimouse opened his eyes there, towering above him, was the spaniel, once again her normal size.

"Woof," she barked, running up and down the street, delighted to be herself once more.

"Woof," replied Septimouse. "Don't forget you'll have a juicy bone on the day of the party. Go and tell the other dogs."

60

"Woof," agreed the spaniel, wagging her tail enthusiastically and running off down the street.

"Good," muttered Septimouse to himself. "Yes, very good. The cheese is being made, the mice have been informed, the cats have been dealt with and a deal has been made with the dogs. Yes, a very good day's work. What an absolutely wonderful mouse I am. Now back to the factory to tell the family that the last problem has been solved by my genius and skill."

The Great Cheese Party

On the day of the Great Cheese Tasting Party, John, James and Julius were busy draping the factory with coloured streamers to make it look festive. Jeremy and Jack were pinning up a banner opposite the mouse entrance, which read:

Welcome to the first mouse cheese factory in the world.

> ## Welcome to the First Mouse Cheese Factory
> ## in the World

Joseph was helping his mother lay out napkins and plates on a long table. Mr Mouse and Septimouse were sampling the cheese.

"Delicious," proclaimed Mr Mouse as he nibbled the cheese. "Though I say so myself, this cheese beats anything I ever smelled in a trap." And he smiled broadly.

"Mmm," agreed Septimouse. "It's not bad, though I daresay we will think of some improvements as we go on."

"Of course," said Mr Mouse, beaming. "But this is excellent as a first try."

"I've forgotten something," exclaimed Septimouse. "We must have an entrance from the street."

"But why?" asked his mother.

"Well, we can't have dozens of mice wandering through my little big person's house. Big big person Dad and big big person Mum might not like it."

"Do you think your friend the dog might dig an entrance for us, leading from the garden?"

"Good thinking, Dad," said Septimouse. "I will go and find that dog and offer her one of the big juicy bones little big person Katie bought."

The dog was very enthusiastic at the thought of earning an extra bone and

began digging energetically. Katie put a
wheelbarrow in front of the dog, just in
case Mum or Dad came by and wondered
what was going on. After a few minutes

the dog had finished. Septimouse and Katie looked at the new entrance and smiled.

"It's wonderful," Katie said.

"Woof, woof, woof, woof," Septimouse translated.

"Woof," agreed the dog, wagging her tail. "Can I have my bone now?"

Katie went and got the bone.

"Woof," said the dog. "Hey, Septimouse, can I come to your party tonight?"

"You want me to shrink you again?"

"Yes, I want to see this cheese factory. Woof, would you promise to make me dog-sized again when it is all over?"

"Woof," agreed Septimouse.

"What's going on?" asked Katie.

"The dog wants to come to the party," Septimouse explained. "And I'm saying all right."

"But I don't understand. How can that big dog go to your party? He'd never get in."

"I can shrink him."

"*Shrink* him!" exclaimed Katie.

"Why, yes. For as you know I am the seventh . . ."

"4S, yes, I do believe you've mentioned it once or twice!"

"Well, one of my 4S magic talents is that

I can shrink things like milk cartons and dogs."

"Could you shrink me? Oh please, Septimouse, please, please, please. I would *so* love to come to your party."

"Of course I will. Now why didn't I think of that myself? Be in the kitchen on the dot of twelve midnight and I will shrink you and personally invite you to be the guest of honour at our grand factory opening."

So at five minutes to twelve, Septimouse stepped out into the kitchen. Katie was waiting in her dressing-gown. Oscar was rubbing himself against her legs. Septimouse closed his eyes tightly and held up his hands.

"Little Katie in a trice,

Be as small as us mice."

He opened his eyes and there was Katie smiling and looking straight into his eyes.

Septimouse grinned and bowed down:

"Little *small* person Katie, pray be my guest of honour at the grand opening of the cheese factory." And he took her hand and led her towards the mouse hole. Suddenly they heard a loud cry.

"Hey, Septimouse, what have you done to poor Katie?"

There stood Oscar towering over them and looking very puzzled and upset.

"Shrunk her, Oscar, so that she could come to our grand opening party."

"What about me?" demanded Oscar. "You're going off to have fun and leaving me here all on my own. It's not fair. Can I be shrunk to mouse size as well and come to the party?"

"Of course, Oscar. I'm sorry. I should have thought of it myself. It's just that I've had so much on these last few days. You have been so helpful, a real friend to mice, of course you must come and be my second honoured guest." And closing his eyes he intoned:

"Oscar, friend to every mouse,
Shrink so that you can enter this house."

In a second Oscar was as small as Katie and Septimouse, and together they walked smiling into the mouse hole. Inside there were mice chatting and laughing and munching cheese. Septimouse climbed on to the table, which was weighed down with cheese, and called out:

"Mice, friends, dear parents, ladies and gentlemen, pray silence for me."

A hush fell.

"Thank you, friends, thank you. I have no wish to stop you eating and enjoying yourselves – that is why you are here, so I

will be brief. First, I want to introduce
three dear friends without whose help
none of you would be at this wonderful
event. Please give a big hand for little big
person Katie, who generously gave her
own money to buy us milk."

The mice clapped heartily as Katie
climbed up next to Septimouse.

"She's not big," cried Jeremy.

"She's no bigger than us," agreed John and James.

"That is because with my amazing magical powers I have shrunk her," explained Septimouse proudly. "So welcome, Katie and, on behalf of all the mice here, thank you for your help in launching this wonderful factory. Three cheers for Katie. Hip, hip . . ."

And three times all the mice joined in the "Hurrah".

"And now welcome to my two other guests and helpers, a dog and Oscar the cat."

"A cat," shrieked the mice, and rushed to hide under the table and behind the curtains.

"Oh come back, come back," shouted Septimouse. "Am I not Septimouse, the seventh son of a seventh son? This splendid cat is my friend and yours and what is more he is as small as you. Come on, Oscar, up on to the table."

Oscar shook his head. "They don't like me," he wept. "The little mice don't like me one bit. I want to go, please make me cat-sized again, Septi, old boy."

"If you mice don't stop being silly and welcome Oscar politely, I will close down the factory," announced Septimouse.

Gradually the mice crept out and looked suspiciously at the weeping Oscar.

"This cat," Septimouse told them sternly, "is a wonderful friend to mice. He has faithfully carried me up to little big person Katie many times and he knew the addresses of every one of you mice so that you could be invited here tonight. So come on, don't be mean to Oscar, he can't help being a cat. Three cheers for Oscar. Hip, hip . . ."

And once more the mice all shouted "Hurrah" three times very enthusiastically.

"That's better," declared Septimouse.

The party went on all night. They ate
and they drank, they danced and they
played games until it began to get light and
the birds started to sing in the trees. Weary
but happy, the mice prepared to go home,
but before they left they all promised to
look for coins to help buy milk.

Septimouse waved them goodbye as they scampered off. He looked at Oscar who was busy helping the mice with the clearing up and the dog who was trying some cheese and Katie who was fast asleep.

"Before I go to sleep myself," he thought, "I must restore them to their normal size. Dog, out you go so that I can make you dog-sized again."

"Woof," agreed the dog, and ran out into the garden.

"Be big again," commanded Septimouse.

"Woof," barked the dog. "Thanks, I had a good time. I'll look out for coins too for my bone. Woof."

"Katie, wake up!" shouted Septimouse.

"Tired," muttered Katie, and went back to sleep.

"Hopeless," sighed Septimouse. "Come on, Oscar, help me carry her out into the kitchen."

"I'll give you a hand," said Mr Mouse, putting down the broom.

"Be very careful," said Mrs Mouse. "Don't drop her whatever you do."

Oscar took Katie's arms and Septimouse and Mr Mouse took a leg each and they carried the girl out into the kitchen. They staggered over to the kitchen table.

"I can't go a step further," panted Oscar.

"This will do," said Septimouse. "You go back home, Father. I'm going to turn Oscar into a full-sized cat again. Go home so that you won't tempt him."

"Don't worry, I'm off," said Mr Mouse, scampering home as fast as he could.

"Oscar and little big person Katie, be big again," intoned Septimouse wearily.

Instantly a full-sized Katie was sleeping peacefully under the kitchen table and Oscar was his normal size.

"Miaow," said Oscar. "Septi, old boy, what will big big person Dad and big big person Mum think when they find Katie asleep on the kitchen floor?"

"I don't know," replied Septimouse, yawning. "But I can't worry about that now. I'm exhausted and I'm going to bed. Even seventh sons of seventh sons get tired occasionally!"